BOY + **BOT**

by **AME DYCKMAN**

illustrated by **DAN YACCARINO**

Alfred A. Knopf 🐕 **New York**

For Alaric, The Boy—A.D.

For Joe Rash—D.Y.

THIS IS A BORZOI BOOK PUBLISHED BY ALFRED A. KNOPF

Text copyright © 2012 by Ame Dyckman

Jacket art and interior illustrations copyright © 2012 by Dan Yaccarino

All rights reserved. Published in the United States by Alfred A. Knopf, an imprint of Random House Children's Books,

a division of Random House, Inc., New York.

Knopf, Borzoi Books, and the colophon are registered trademarks of Random House, Inc.

Visit us on the Web! www.randomhouse.com/kids

Educators and librarians, for a variety of teaching tools, visit us at www.randomhouse.com/teachers

Library of Congress Cataloging-in-Publication Data

Dyckman, Ame.

Boy and Bot / by Ame Dyckman ; illustrated by Dan Yaccarino. — 1st ed.

p. cm.

ISBN 978-0-375-86756-9 (trade) — ISBN 978-0-375-96757-3 (lib. bdg.) — ISBN 978-0-375-98724-3 (ebook)

SUMMARY: A boy and a robot strike up a friendship despite their differences.

[1. Robots—Fiction. 2. Friendship—Fiction.] I. Yaccarino, Dan, ill. II. Title.

PZ7.D9715Bo 2012

[E]—dc23

2011016682

The illustrations in this book were created using gouache on watercolor paper.

MANUFACTURED IN CHINA

April 2012   10 9 8 7 6 5 4 3 2   First Edition

A boy was collecting pinecones in his wagon when he met a robot.

"Hi!" said the boy. "Want to play?"
The robot blinked. "Affirmative!"

They played. They had fun.

But as they rolled down the hill, a rock bumped
the robot's power switch and the robot turned off.
"What's wrong?" the boy asked.

The robot did not answer. "Are you sick?" the boy asked.

The robot still did not answer.

"I must help him," the boy said.

The boy fed him applesauce.

He took the robot home.

He read the robot a story.

And he tucked him in.
"Good night, Bot," the boy whispered,
and climbed into bed.

Later, the boy's parents peeked in on him.
They did not see Bot behind the door. The
door bumped Bot on his power switch.
BEEP! Bot turned on.

"What-is-wrong?" Bot asked.

The boy did not answer.

"Did-you-malfunction?" Bot asked.

The boy still did not answer. "I-must-help-him," Bot said.

Bot gave him oil.

He took the boy home.

He read the boy an instruction manual.

He was bringing him a spare battery
when the Inventor walked in.

"Stop!" the Inventor shouted. "That is a *boy*!"

The boy woke with a start. Then he saw Bot.
The boy smiled. "Bot! You are cured!"

Bot lit up. "Boy! You-are-fixed!"
The Inventor called Boy's parents.

Then he drove Boy home.

"Good night, Bot," Boy said.

"Good-night-Boy," Bot said. "Want-to-play-tomorrow?"

Boy nodded. "Affirmative!"

And the friends did.